One Frozen Lake

One FROZEN Lake

Deborah Jo Larson

Paintings by **Steve Johnson** and **Lou Fancher**

Minnesota Historical Society Press

One frozen lake.
Two fishing friends.

Three bundles packed with
Line, lures, and snacks.

Four frosty inches.

Splash!

ORIGINAL
DEPT. OF CONSERVATION   STATE OF MINNESOTA   DIV. O
FEE $1.50   1958 No. A 2
RESIDENT INDIVIDUAL FISHING LICENSE

Five hours pass.
Not one fish.

Where are the fish?

One frozen lake.
One warm, canvas shack.

Two new jig sticks
For two fishing friends.

Three trays of tackle
Sinkers, spoons, and spins.

Four watery holes
Tunnels to peek in.

Ooooh.

Five more shacks
New fishing friends.

Six cups of cocoa
Warm bellies and hands.

Mmmmm.

Seven hours pass.

Not one fish.
Has *anyone* seen a fish?

One pink sun
Finds one frozen lake.

Two busy friends
Mark, drill, and scrape.

Reels and Baits.

Three-foot drop-off—
Here, Mister Pike!

Jig, jig, jig . . .

Four lost leeches
Five failed rigs.

Six-pound test line.
SNAP! Nothing!

Sigh.
Gimme all your sevens.
Go fish.
Eights?

Nine o'clock. Already?
Better reel in.

Wiggle-wiggle.

Wait . . .
A fish?

A fish!
Ten inches!
A keeper!
Yeah!

Flip, flop.

"Um, Grandpa . . ."

"No, really?"

"Please . . ."

Splash!

One frozen lake, good-bye.
Two fishing friends, good night.

Three miles 'til home, sweet dreams.

Another lake,
Another day,
Another fish.

To Jim, Luke, Alex, Mom, Dad, Julia, Barb K., and Barb W.
You are all keepers!

Love always, Deb

www.mhspress.org

Manufactured in Canada

10 9 8 7 6 5 4 3 2 1

♾ The paper used in this publication meets the minimum requirements of the American National Standard for Information Sciences—Permanence for Printed Library Materials, ANSI Z39.48-1984.

International Standard Book Number
ISBN: 978-0-87351-866-6 (cloth)

LIBRARY OF CONGRESS
CATALOGING-IN-PUBLICATION DATA

Larson, Deborah Jo.
One frozen lake / Deborah Jo Larson ; illustrations by Steve Johnson and Lou Fancher.
pages cm
Summary: "Grandpa introduces grandchild to the art of ice fishing—sharing a cozy ice shack, sorting colorful tackle, and finding ways to pass the time. But where are the fish? Will they ever catch a fish?"— Provided by publisher.
ISBN 978-0-87351-866-6 (cloth : alk. paper)
[1. Ice fishing—Fiction. 2. Fishing—Fiction. 3. Grandfathers—Fiction. 4. Counting.] I. Johnson, Steve, 1960– illustrator. II. Fancher, Lou, illustrator. III. Title.
PZ7.L32386On 2012
[E]—dc23
2012022470

First published in the U.S. in 1989 by Ideals Publishing Corporation,
Nashville, Tennessee 37214

Copyright © 1989 by Templar Publishing Co. Ltd.
Illustrations copyright © 1989 by Templar Publishing Co. Ltd.

Printed and bound by MacLehose & Partners Ltd., United Kingdom

Library of Congress Cataloging-in-Publication Data
McCaughrean, Geraldine.
    The story of Christmas.

    Summary: A retelling of the events leading up to and
following the birth of Jesus Christ.
    1. Jesus Christ—Nativity—Juvenile literature.
[1. Jesus Christ—Nativity.   2. Bible stories—N.T.]
I. Ward, Helen, 1962-   ill.   II. Title.
BT315.2.M337   1989   232.92   89-11048
ISBN 0-8249-8385-8

THE STORY OF

CHRISTMAS

told by Geraldine McCaughrean
illustrated by Helen Ward

IDEALS CHILDREN'S BOOKS
Nashville, Tennessee

From the very beginning, God knew. And when it was time, he lighted a new star in the sky to mark the beginning. Then he gave the Angel Gabriel a message to deliver.

As Zacharias, a priest in the temple in Jerusalem, stood in the holiest part of the temple one day, an angel appeared to him with the message. "I have great news for you, Zacharias," he said. "Your wife, Elizabeth, is going to have a baby boy."

"Surely not!" exclaimed Zacharias. "All our lives we have wanted children, and none have come. Now we are both far too old."

But the angel insisted. "You must call him John. He will be a great man with the power to make people stop and listen. He will tell the world of another who is coming; he will be like a trumpeter before a king."

Frightened and amazed, Zacharias stumbled out of the temple. But when he tried to talk to the people around him, even Elizabeth, he found he could not. The angel had taken away his voice.

Elizabeth had a cousin called Mary who lived in Nazareth. Mary was a good person, honest and kind, modest and generous.

Mary was promised in marriage to Joseph the carpenter; but one morning a few weeks before the wedding, the Angel Gabriel appeared to her too. He said, "Greetings, Mary! Do not be afraid.

"Today a new life will begin in you, for God has chosen you to be the mother of Jesus – the savior of the world."

"But how?" asked Mary in amazement.

"God who made the world will strike the spark of life in you," replied the angel.

And Mary bowed her head in acceptance of this message. Although this was a hard task, Mary loved God and always did as he wanted.

When Joseph found out that Mary was expecting a baby, he was upset and confused.

"How can this be?" Joseph said to himself. "How can I possibly marry her now?" And Joseph decided that he could not take Mary as his wife.

But that night as Joseph slept, an angel came to him in a dream.

"Joseph!" the angel said. "Don't break your promise to Mary. You would have to go to the end of the world to find a better woman than Mary. Don't worry. Marry her . . . and be happy. The baby she is expecting is Jesus, the savior of the world."

So Joseph wedded Mary – and was happy and proud too.

Soon after Mary heard the Angel Gabriel's message, she set out to visit her cousin Elizabeth.

"God has blessed us, Mary," Elizabeth said. "But most of all, he has blessed you. Of all the women in the world, he has chosen you to be the mother of someone more wonderful than we can imagine. The baby inside me leaps and dances now that he is close to yours. From now until the end of time, people are going to thank you for giving birth to our Lord."

Soon afterward, Elizabeth's son was born; and Zacharias's house was full of friends and neighbors who had come to see the baby.

"What are you going to call him, Zacharias?" they asked. But Zacharias still could not speak, so he wrote down his answer: "HIS NAME IS JOHN."

At that moment, God gave Zacharias back his voice, and he could shout from the rooftops, "His name is John! His name is John!"

Such a special baby, such a miraculous son – this baby John! The neighbors could not help but wonder if John were going to be the savior promised to them in the holy Scriptures.

But John was not the savior. He was only a messenger preparing the way.

Far away in Rome, Emperor Caesar Augustus ruled a mighty empire which stretched as far as the eye could see and beyond. He had power over the lives of men, women, and children in countries he had never seen – in towns and villages from the edge of the desert to the shores of the sea. And when the emperor spoke, people the whole world over listened and obeyed.

That year he ordered everyone, wherever they were, whatever they were doing, to travel to their place of birth to be counted and to pay a tax to the empire. Even though it was almost time for their baby to be born, Joseph and Mary set off for the little town of Bethlehem, in Judea, where Joseph had been born.

It was a long and wearisome journey.

A cruel and greedy king ruled in Judea at that time. His name was Herod.

One day three wise and wealthy philosophers arrived at the gates of Herod's palace. "We have come to see the newborn king," they said, "the mighty savior. We have seen his star shining in the east – and have come to worship him."

A new king? thought Herod. Why, only I and my sons shall ever rule this land!

Herod called his scribes to him, and they told him of the scriptures which foretold a great savior being born in Bethlehem.

Herod hid his anger and said to the wise men, "The baby isn't here. You must follow your star a little further, it would seem. But please promise me that you will come back and tell me where the king is . . . so that I too may pay my respects."

The three wise men promised to do so and continued on their way.

Bethlehem was milling with people when Mary and Joseph arrived. Every man born there had returned to be counted, bringing his wife and children with him.

Joseph knocked at one inn, but the landlord poked his head out and said, "No room! Every bed is taken. No room!"

Joseph knocked at door after door, but the answer was always the same – no room.

"But the time has almost come for my wife to have her baby," said Joseph, leaning wearily against the doorpost of the very last inn.

"No room! No room!" said the innkeeper. "Unless . . ."

And he led them to a stable full of the steamy breath and strong, sweet smell of animals.

There the innkeeper gave Mary and Joseph straw to lie on and a lantern to fend off the darkness.

So that is where Mary's baby was born. She called him Jesus and laid him in a manger on a soft, golden bed of straw.

Only the animals saw the birth, blinking their dark eyes and nodding their heads and silently chewing. It looked almost as if they were speaking to one another.

"He has come at last," they seemed to say. "Jesus the savior is born."

Not far from that joyful scene, a group of
shepherds, wrapped in their cloaks, kept watch
over their flocks of sheep.

Overhead a sea of stars stretched from one end
of the sky to the other.

Suddenly, an angel of the Lord appeared before the shepherds. They were terrified.

"Do not be afraid," said the angel. "I've come to bring you good news. A baby is born tonight in a stable in Bethlehem. His name is Jesus – savior of the world. All heaven is celebrating his arrival tonight."

And suddenly, a great host of angels appeared shouting, "Glory to God! Peace to his people on earth!"

They soared higher and higher, until they were no more than sparks of light among the stars.

"What news to be told to us!" cried one of the shepherds.

"Let's go and see this miracle," said a second. "Let's go and see this baby!"

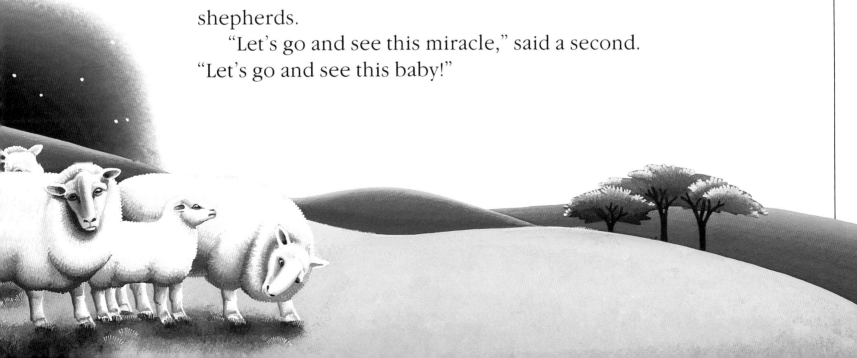

Meanwhile, the three wise men had been following the course of a bright, new star across the night sky for many miles. Now it stood still over the stable of an inn. Had there not been a light burning inside, they might easily have shrugged their shoulders and gone away.

Ducking inside, they found a man, a woman, and a group of shepherds. The wise men knelt in front of the wooden manger because they had also found the newborn king whose star had begun their journey.

"I give you gold," said one, "because you are the King of Kings."

"Frankincense, the sweet smell of the temple," said the second, "because I know you are holy."

"Myrrh, a perfume for the grave," said the third sadly, "because you will die all too soon."

As the three wise philosophers slept contentedly that night, an angel came to them in their dreams.

"Do not go back to King Herod," he said, "for the king is a cruel and jealous man who should not know of the baby's whereabouts."

When the three men awoke, they found they had all shared the same dream. They quickly saddled their camels and hurried homeward by another road.

Herod, meanwhile, was growing angry. "What's keeping them?" he shouted. "Why don't they return?" Then a dark and silent wickedness settled over the king.

He decreed that all baby boys in Bethlehem two years of age and under be killed. "Then I and my sons shall wear the crown of Judea forever!" he declared.

But that night as Joseph slept, an angel appeared to him and said, "Wake up, Joseph, and wake your wife. Herod's soldiers are coming with murder in their hearts and blood on their hands. Leave Bethlehem. Leave Judea. Run for Egypt and hide there until the danger is past!"

So Joseph and Mary fled beyond the reach of the Roman Empire, into the desert land of Egypt. They fled beyond the reach of Herod and his soldiers and their sharp swords.

In his fury, Herod scoured the land for the baby king, and much blood and many tears were spilled. But all that Herod found was hatred in the eyes of his people.

Years went by before Mary and Joseph returned to Nazareth with their baby son – Jesus, our savior.

"Where have you been?" the neighbors asked. "What happened to you?" And they would say nothing – but simply think about the things in their hearts and remember.

Far away in Bethlehem, the little stable was quiet once more, except for the nodding, chewing, and breathing of the animals over the straw-filled manger.

Outside the stars had paled, the hoofprints of the camels had faded, and the shepherds had long since gone back to their sheep.

But the sights and sounds of that night – the night of the birth of our Lord, the first Christmas – were written in the memories of all the visitors to the little stable in Bethlehem.

And high up – too high
and too far off for anyone
to hear – the angels were
still singing.